Christmas
2024 ♡

CH00840326

This book belongs to

...... Zainab ......

..... with lots of love .....

at Christmas

from your father's friend,

Emma (Jumpse)

& Jim (dog)

PUFFIN BOOKS

UK | USA | Canada | Ireland | Australia | India | New Zealand | South Africa

Puffin Books is part of the Penguin Random House group of companies
whose addresses can be found at global.penguinrandomhouse.com.

First published in hardback 2022
This paperback edition published 2024
001

Printed in China

The authorized representative in the EEA is Penguin Random House Ireland,
Morrison Chambers, 32 Nassau Street, Dublin D02 YH68

A CIP catalogue record for this book is available from the British Library
ISBN: 978–0–241–48890–4

All correspondence to: Puffin Books, Penguin Random House Children's
One Embassy Gardens, 8 Viaduct Gardens, London SW11 7BW

Supporting the world's leading museum of art and design,
the Victoria and Albert Museum, London

MIX
Paper | Supporting
responsible forestry
FSC® C018179

Penguin Random House is committed to a
sustainable future for our business, our readers
and our planet. This book is made from Forest
Stewardship Council® certified paper.

Picture Credits

Endpapers: Based on a wallpaper design for Jackson & Graham by Owen Jones, pencil and
bodycolour on paper, UK, c.1860, V&A: D.736-1897 © Victoria and Albert Museum, London

p. 74: Sir Henry Cole, cartoon by Carlo Pellegrini, published in *Vanity Fair*, colour lithograph,
Great Britain, 1871, V&A: E.2178-1932 © Victoria and Albert Museum, London

p. 75: Jim at Broadstairs by Sir Henry Cole, etching, 1864, V&A: 26471:4
© Victoria and Albert Museum, London

p. 75: Commemorative plaque for Jim, pet dog of Sir Henry Cole, in the John Madejski Garden
of the V&A © Stuart Cox, Victoria and Albert Museum, London

Jim's Spectacular Christmas

WRITTEN BY

Emma Thompson

ILLUSTRATED BY

Axel Scheffler

 V&A

This is **Jim**.

He is a **Dog**.

You may feel that I am in danger
of stating the obvious; however, Jim
has been taken, on occasion, for:

1. an old mop-head,

2. a caterpillar,

3. a hairy mushroom.

Jim was not a glamorous animal. He had a bald patch on his left leg, lop-sided ears, a gamey whiff about him, and a rheumy eye, through which he could see very little.

These disadvantages notwithstanding, Jim happened — extraordinarily — to live in a grand museum, in a very smart London district.

How he got there is anybody's guess. The story went
that, back in the days when sending small children
up chimneys to clean them was beginning to be
frowned upon, an enterprising sweep named Josiah
Gargle hit upon the idea of tying Jim to the end of his
brush and pushing him up the chimney, instead of
his unfortunate apprentice, Ernie, who had grown
too long for the purpose.

One remarkable day, while sweeping the chimneys of a grand museum, the twine holding Jim to the brush end snapped and Jim escaped.

He ran about the choking, labyrinthine flues for some long, unpleasant moments before skidding and sliding down a very wide and sudden chimney into a very wide and sudden fireplace.

Luckily, it being summer and the fire unlit,
the worst consequences were the depositing of a
quantity of soot over the assembled company and the
attaching of a number of pointy decorative teazles to
Jim's person.

A rather portly gentleman with a wild shock of white
hair suggested that Jim be washed and brought back.

After several dunkings, latherings, scrubbings and
rinsings, all unwelcome, Jim was returned looking
exactly the same.

The portly gentleman covered in soot turned out to be none other than **Sir Henry Cole**, the director of the museum. Josiah Gargle was brought forth, babbling his apologies and offering to beat Jim soundly for his crimes.

Sir Henry, having been soundly beaten himself while at school, turned down this kind offer and instead stated his intention of keeping Jim, on the condition that Mr Gargle agree not to beat Ernie or any person or animal ever again.

So it was that Jim began his life as a **Museum Dog**.

This museum was a marvel of construction.
It had avenues, piazzas, porticoes, galleries, courts,
balconies, vistas, streets, pavilions, passages, piers,
pagodas, palatial staircases, arches, domes, spires,
gardens, fountains, balustrades and seventy-five loos.

To Jim, it was
the **entire world**.

Sir Henry was well fed, kind and had all his own hair – to Jim, he was everything you could possibly want in an owner.

He followed Sir Henry wherever he went, and as something was forever being built in the museum, this meant the pair of them often walked many miles a day.

Sir Henry constantly needed to send messages to his
builders, his engineers, his artists and his hairdresser,
and he took to using Jim as a post-dog. Jim, whose
sense of direction had been finely honed in the
chimney flues of his youth, found it easy to navigate
the several buildings, and on the way he often visited
his favourite scenes, places and characters.

There were many other dogs in the museum, mostly made of paint. Jim's favourite was a friendly but sad-looking creature, which sat at the feet of a young man holding an artist's palette and a paintbrush. Jim would often sit and bark at the dog until museum staff complained and Sir Henry would be sent for.

"You can bark all you like, he won't hear you!"

said Sir Henry time and again, but Jim refused to believe him.

The dog looked so real. Jim felt sure that if he tried hard enough it would hear him and come to play.

12

When Jim was not barking at the painted dog or delivering post, he indulged in his favourite pastime, which was reading. He was a great reader.

He was fond of plays, loved histories, viewed poetry with respectful terror, adored biographies, devoured mysteries, lapped up histories, thrilled at ghost stories, swallowed novels, passionately favoured anything to do with the animal kingdom and generally regarded literature of every variety as his personal and private domain. There was only one thing troubling him. His only good eye was beginning to go a little fuzzy.

The rheumy one had never been any use, so Jim had been long accustomed to reading with one eye, with a paw over the other. It had never held him back until this moment. But now, he clearly needed spectacles. Or, to be precise, a spec.

That being an impossibility, Jim simply had to hope that his good eye would hold out for as long as possible.

One day, as Christmas was approaching, Sir Henry
was bounding about the latest building site and, as was
his wont, making little notes and drawings in his
notepad, when he came upon a group of builders
having their tea break. He stopped short. He looked
intently at the builders, who were having such a nice
time chatting and cracking jokes that they did not
notice him. Jim watched as Sir Henry cocked his head
to one side. Jim cocked his head to the same side but
could see nothing out of the ordinary.

Sir Henry made a sketch in his notepad and thoughtfully withdrew to his study, where he drew at his desk for a long time. Jim was intrigued. His master, normally boiling with activity, sat quietly at his desk for a good hour, simply scribbling.

Finally, Sir Henry looked up at Jim, his eyes bright with creation.

"**Well, Jim,**" he said.

"**What do you think of this?**"

He showed Jim what he had been drawing. It was in the same shape and arrangement as the group of builders at their tea, but Sir Henry had replaced them with family members – a mother, a father and a group of children, with everyone holding a glass, looking happily out at the viewer.

Beneath the drawing was the legend:

A MERRY CHRISTMAS
AND
A HAPPY NEW YEAR
TO YOU

Jim thought it was artful and very much gave the impression of festive cheer. He yelped his approval.

"**Yes**," said Sir Henry. "**Yes, that's what I thought. And if I were to add a little something on either side — showing people being kind to those less fortunate, do you think this is something we might be able to send to our friends as a gift?**"

Jim licked Sir Henry's hand in agreement.

"*Good. I'm glad you agree,*" said Sir Henry, wiping his hand on his trouser leg.

He wrote a note on the back of his drawing and gave it to Jim. "*Take this to Horsley for me and wait for the reply.*"

Jim trotted through the buildings to the office of **John Horsley**, who was an artist. Jim went back and forth many times between the two friends until Sir Henry was satisfied with the final result.

It looked something like this.

A MERRY CHRISTMAS
AND
A HAPPY NEW YEAR
TO YOU

From

Sir Henry became more and more excited. He loved sending things by post and indeed had invented his very own Universal Postal Service, which had stamps and everything.

But at Christmas he was much oppressed by the massive quantity of greetings that needed to be sent, all handwritten and all wishing people the same thing — a happy Christmas.

He thought that a Christmas Card, as he called it, printed with the sentiments he wished to express would be just as welcome, and save him and Lady Cole a great deal of time and effort. Accordingly, he printed one thousand copies of his new creation and made a list of all the people he wanted to send them to.

"**I do think it could catch on,**" he said to Jim, as they trotted towards the recently completed refreshments parlour for Sir Henry's seventh coffee and Jim's morning bowl of custard.

"**But we must find a way to popularize it. Let me see.**
        Who is the most popular person in all the land?"

Jim thought the answer must be Sir Henry and barked to signify his opinion.

"**Ah, you're a faithful old fellow, Jim,**" said Sir Henry, whose good opinion of himself ran almost as high as Jim's. "**But no, not enough people know of me —
this must be someone EVERYONE knows of . . .**"

He paused for a moment beneath a portrait of . . .

Queen Victoria!

Sir Henry slapped a hand to his forehead.

"By gosh and golly, that's it! We shall send the Christmas Card to Her Majesty! And she will tell everyone in the land all about it!"

Sir Henry was giddy with excitement. Jim ran back
and forth between him and John Horsley with new
versions of the Christmas Card until he was quite
worn out. As he lay at his master's feet, Sir Henry
stared down at him lovingly.

"*What a good post-dog you are, Jim.*"
And his eyes lit up. "*By gosh and golly,
that's it!* **YOU** *shall deliver the Card
to Her Majesty! You, Jim!*"

Jim opened his good eye and
stared at Sir Henry in disbelief.

"**Yes!** *I shall send you in a carriage upon a
cushion of velvet! With a golden collar and
you shall carry the Card to Queen Victoria.*"

Suddenly Jim didn't feel tired at all. He sprang up!
He – Jim, the sweep's mongrel – **HE** was to be
admitted to the presence of the Queen of England.

He was so excited he was **sick**.

When the day of the grand delivery came, Jim endured a thorough wash and two hours with Sir Henry's hairdresser. He was appalled at the result. But nevertheless nothing could dim the thrill of the small carriage that awaited him, with the tasselled velvet cushion upon which he was to sit.

Sir Henry plied him with so many instructions on Royal Protocol that it made his good eye swim. In the end, the only thing Jim could remember was not to drool upon the envelope.

The Christmas Card was placed inside the carriage next to Jim, who was in turn placed upon the cushion. It made its grand way through the streets of Albertopolis to the great gates of Buckingham Palace. Jim's heart swelled and fluttered and soared like one of the kites he could see in Hyde Park.

The carriage passed through the gates, past the guards and the rollicking crowds of tourists and daytrippers, all eager to know what grand personage was within, and were consequently very confused by the sight of a small dog with tonged hair on a cushion.

At last, the carriage stopped under the portico. Jim took the Christmas Card in his mouth, holding it away from his tongue with his teeth.

A steward opened the door and picked up Jim's cushion. Jim winked at the steward but got no response, which confused him because all the staff at the museum were so friendly. But, he supposed, this was Buckingham Palace, and the rules must be different.

The steward took him up a magnificent staircase covered in rich ruby-red carpet and along a great hall filled with shining armour, and then another filled with paintings, and yet another filled with massive gilt furniture.

There were other stewards and guards in all these halls and many frock-coated gentlemen carrying papers and looking important. It was another world.

Jim stared and stared while also trying to keep his balance on the cushion. The steward was young and had a sprightly gait.

Finally, they entered a room that appeared to be full of children. There were many nurses too and it was a moment before, through the crowd, Jim saw an image that would remain with him for the rest of his days.

The Queen, for surely it must be she, crowned, tiny and round, had clearly spilled something like tea down her front, and Prince Albert, for it must surely be he, was dabbing it away with his pocket handkerchief.

The scene, so domestic, comforting and at odds with all Jim's expectations, quite overcame his nerves. They were just like normal humans! He relaxed everything except his salivary glands.

Within moments he was placed ceremoniously at the Queen's feet, the steward stepped back and Prince Albert, with much amusement, said:

"What have we here?" in an accent like nothing Jim had ever heard before.

As instructed by Sir Henry, Jim stood and walked carefully off the cushion, the Christmas Card still between his teeth. Bowing low over his forepaws, he then got on to his hind legs and offered the Card to the Queen. Her large eyes popped even wider and she laughed as she took the Card from Jim's mouth and opened it.

"*Ah, but how delightful!*" she cried.

"**Look, my love!**" And she handed it to Prince Albert.

Prince Albert took an object from his pocket and fitted it to his eye. It was a monocle. Like Jim, he was short-sighted in one eye.

Jim stared.

It was a 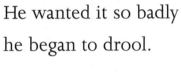**spec**.

It was **EXACTLY** what he needed.

He must have it.

He wanted it so badly

he began to drool.

The steward noticed and removed him unceremoniously from the Royal feet.

"Come and see this wonderful picture, children!" cried the Queen, and a great crowd of nurses, toddlers, children and babies enveloped her. Prince Albert took one of the babies from its nurse's arms.

"Come and see the Christmas Card" he said. The baby was far more interested in his monocle, which it plucked from the Royal eye and put into its mouth.

Jim jealously watched the journey of the monocle and his heart leapt when Prince Albert took it out of the baby's fat little fist and put it down on a side table.

Jim skulked around the family group towards the table. It was small but very high. He stared hungrily up at the spec. Perhaps if he were to leap . . . Suddenly there was a low growl.

A very portly corgi was lying just beyond the table, staring at Jim with contempt.

"Hello," said Jim,
his mind racing.

"*What've you come as, sonny boy?*" said the corgi in strangulated tones. "*A May-Day Dainty?*"

Jim snorted back at him.

"*What on earth do they feed you, Pork Belly?*"

"**Eh?**" said the ancient, spoiled old creature.

"*I bet you can't even make it to the door without being picked up,*" jeered Jim.

The corgi, enraged, rose unsteadily and charged at Jim straight through the legs of the side table, which tipped over.

Jim easily outmanoeuvred the portly dog and caught the monocle as it flew through the air, clamping his jaws around it and running from the room. The old dog barked and the children laughed to see their pet chasing off the new, manicured arrival.

Jim raced back down the three galleries, past the gilt furniture, past the oil paintings and past the armour. He raced past the guards and straight through the open carriage door and out of the other side.

He ran pell-mell down Pall Mall.

Panting, he reached Hyde Park and slowed to a trot.
He knew London and he knew Albertopolis, so he
trotted homewards with the monocle safely stowed
under his tongue.

When he arrived back at the museum, he was in almost as bedraggled a state as when Sir Henry first saw him. As soon as he stepped foot inside the museum, Sir Henry found him.

"**Jim, my boy!**" he yelled, scooping Jim up into his arms. "**I've heard from the Palace already! They sent over such a smart steward! Bless you, my lad! The Queen's full of it! She loves the Christmas Card and she is very sorry the old General chased you off! She says —**"

And here Sir Henry referred to a note in his hand that bore the Royal seal and was signed with a flourish.

"**— she says, yes, look here; she says if there is any way I can make it up to your little messenger, please let me know!**"

Sir Henry gave Jim an almighty hug and put him down.

"I hope you're proud of yourself, Jim. I certainly am.
Now you have a good rest, my boy. You deserve it!"

Sir Henry rushed off to deliver the good news about the Christmas Card to John Horsley, the artist, while Jim crept to the library, the monocle still under his tongue.

Under a chair, he dried it by rubbing it along the carpet with his paws.

Then, shiveringly, he placed it over his eye and opened his book, which was more of a monograph really, entitled: *The Ways of the Mongrel*.

Oh, Glory be!
Oh, let joy be unconfined!
Jim could SEE! He could READ again!

He was completely and entirely happy.
He spent what remained of the day poring over his favourite books until finally, quite exhausted, he lay beneath Sir Henry's armchair and fell asleep.

In the wee small hours, something woke Jim up.

What was it?

Was it a noise?

Jim sat up and listened.

Something about the way his heart was beating didn't feel quite right. Something about the way he was breathing felt somehow out of kilter.

He coughed and shook himself. He lay down and tried to get back to sleep. He couldn't.

In all his years, Jim had never ever had trouble sleeping. He could sleep anywhere and for as long as he liked. He was, in fact, a champion sleeper. But now here he was in the middle of the night, wide awake and with no prospect of being anything other than wide awake.

Confused, he tried to read, but the room was too dark. Thinking there might be more light elsewhere, he put the monocle under his tongue and pattered off with the pamphlet between his teeth.

Even in the dark, Jim knew the galleries and passages of the museum so well that he had no trouble finding his way towards the new refreshments parlour, which had such large windows he thought he might be able to read by the light of the moon.

As he came down one of his favourite corridors, he suddenly heard a soft bark.

He froze.

"Good grief," he thought. **"Has that portly old corgi followed me here?"**

Sweating slightly, he turned. But there was nothing to be seen. No living creature stirred.

Jim's hackles rose. But, seeing nothing, he turned to continue his journey.

Another bark came, this time slightly louder. A pleading sort of bark.

Jim put his pamphlet down and went towards the noise. The pleading bark came once again and now Jim knew exactly where it was coming from.

He looked up to face the painted dog, his silent friend who stood next to the young man with the artist's palette.

"Hello, Jim," said the painted dog in a friendly tone.
"Heddo," said Jim, with difficulty, the monocle now lodged in his cheek.

"**Spit it out, why don't you?**" said the painted dog. Jim, overwhelmed with emotions he did not fully understand, deposited the soggy monocle on the floor.

"**You can't keep it, you know,**" said the painted dog. "**You can't keep it for it is a stolen good.**"

Jim sat and stared at the painted dog.

"**I've just borrowed it,**" he said defensively.

The painted dog gave him a sorrowful look. "**No. It is stolen. You will suffer. Guilt is a terrible thing. I took my master's ham-bone once, when he was hungrier than me. It made me sad. My master painted me after that, which is why I look sad all the time.**"

Jim said, "**But I NEED it.**"

"It doesn't matter," said the dog. "**If you do not give it back, you will never sleep again.**"

Jim thought this sounded like a terrible punishment.

"*Will you give it back?*" asked the dog plaintively.

Jim swallowed.

"*I shall*," he said.

The painted dog gave a little nod, as much of relief as approval, Jim thought. Then Jim looked down at the monocle and with great regret scooped it into his mouth.

He looked up at his new friend.

"*Wash your name?*" he said.

But the painted dog had fallen silent. It looked to Jim as though it might be a little less sad than before.

Jim went slowly back to Sir Henry's study. There he sat, outside the door, for the remainder of the night, unable to sleep, slumping with fatigue first to one side and then the other until his poor neck ached abominably.

And that was where Sir Henry found him the following morning, leaning against the study door in the furthest reaches of exhaustion.

Sir Henry was in his usual state of distraction and at first did not notice Jim's sorry state.

"**Oddest thing, Jim old thing,**" he said, waving the pamphlet on mongrels at Jim. "**I found this lying near the refreshments parlour. No idea how it got there — most peculiar. Hang on — Jim! Jim, look at you! My dear fellow, what on earth is the matter?**"

For reply, Jim simply spat the monocle out at Sir Henry's feet and retreated from him, looking miserably guilty.

Sir Henry peered down at the wet monocle in
confusion. Then he pulled a hankie from one of
many pockets and picked it up, wiped it and
examined it carefully.

He frowned. Jim whined in distress.

"Found this, did you, my boy?"

Jim whined again and retreated even further.

"From the Palace, is it?" said Sir Henry.

Jim covered his head in shame.

Sir Henry seemed to understand immediately
and nodded to himself grimly.

*"Well, we shall return this to its rightful owner without
pause. Or paws."*

And off he went, leaving Jim without another word.

As soon as the monocle left Jim's ownership, his sense of guilt lifted and he fell fast asleep exactly where he was.

Several hours later he was woken by Sir Henry picking him up and plonking him in front of a large bowl of custard.

"The Palace were very understanding," he said. **"There are no bones broken and no hard feelings. So we shall put it behind us, Jim old boy, there's a good dog."**

Jim barked.

"Yes, good fellow. Now come with me, for it's nearly Christmas and there are a thousand Cards to deliver!"

Jim spent the rest of the day carrying the new Christmas Cards to everyone in the building. The oohs and aahs that accompanied their opening rocked the rafters. The Christmas Card was an enormous success.

When Christmas Day dawned, the builders and artists and engineers and architects were all at home and Jim's world was eerily quiet.

But Sir Henry and his family always gave such a jolly Christmas feast and Jim was offered so many greasy scraps of turkey and bacon that by the end of the affair he could barely move.

The time came to hand out gifts. Jim lay in front of the fire snoozing, for the business of present-giving did not involve him and generally took the generous Cole family several hours.

Sir Henry stood in front of the Christmas tree
and demanded everyone's attention.

*"My dears and beloveds — this is a Very Special Christmas,
for a Very Special Member of the family has received a
Very Special Gift indeed!"*

Everyone looked at everyone else, wondering who
it could be.

*"I shall give you a clue as to the recipient of this
Extraordinary Honour — it is the HAIRIEST member of
our family."*

Everyone pointed at Sir Henry, who indeed had more
hair than anyone else in the room.

*"Not me. No. Another clue! The hairiest member
with the most legs!"*

Everyone was very confused. They started to count each other's legs. However, no one appeared to have any more than two.

But then the youngest Cole, a promising child with an interest in mathematics, pointed at Jim, who was still snoozing.

"Jim's hairy and he has FOUR legs!"

Sir Henry crowed with delight.
"It's Jim!" he shouted, picking Jim up and waking him so suddenly that Jim got severe hiccups. Sir Henry held him aloft.

"Our Jim has received a GIFT from none other than our own monarch. From Queen Victoria herself!"

A gasp went round the room. Everyone stared at Jim, which made him feel extremely uncomfortable. He hiccupped violently.

Sir Henry put Jim on his lap and showed him the most beautiful little box, all marked with the Royal insignia and a small card sealed with wax that was imprinted with the Royal seal.

"I shall open this for you, Jim, *so we can all see what she has sent you.*"

Jim could hardly contain himself and could certainly not contain his hiccups. Everyone crowded around as Sir Henry opened the card. He read it aloud.

"**For Jim,**" it said. "*A wonderful post-dog, with gratitude and admiration always from Victoria and Albert.*"

It was too astonishing. The family dog had been sent a present by the Queen of England.

Sir Henry opened the little box. There, nestling on a tiny velvet cushion inside the box, was a very small monocle.

A spec.

Jim's hiccups instantly ceased. Sir Henry placed the monocle over Jim's eye. It fitted perfectly. He could see. He could see so clearly that he nearly fell off Sir Henry's lap. He barked with sheer joy and the room erupted with a great cheer.

Sir Henry whispered into Jim's ear: **"When I returned it, they said they wanted you to have one of your own! They had it specially made just for you!"** Jim turned and licked Sir Henry's face with such abandon that Sir Henry hurriedly put him back down on the floor.

Everyone congratulated Jim, read the card over and over and exclaimed at the honour bestowed upon the entire family.

It was a Christmas that none of them would ever forget.

As the family continued with their gifts, Jim slipped away.

He skittered along the empty, silent corridors, passages, galleries and balconies until he came to the picture of his friend, the painted dog.

For a long time that day he sat under the picture in exactly the same position, proudly wearing his monocle and feeling he was the luckiest, happiest Dog in all of Albertopolis.

The End

About the real-life **Jim**

Jim really was a **museum dog!**

For most of his life he lived at the **South Kensington Museum**, now the Victoria and Albert Museum, as the faithful terrier companion of **Sir Henry Cole**, the museum's director. The two friends were so often seen together that a caricature of Cole published in 1871 shows Jim just behind Cole, perched inquisitively up on his hind legs.

Illustration of Sir Henry Cole & Jim

When Jim lived in the area now known as South Kensington, there were lots of new museums and colleges being built. According to an architectural journal called *The Builder*, Henry and Jim would tour the building sites together early in the morning and could be seen clambering over bricks and girders, up ladders and about scaffolding, inspecting all that was going on.

At the time, this area was nicknamed **Albertopolis** after **Prince Albert**. Prince Albert and Henry Cole worked together on **The Great Exhibition of 1851**, the world's first international display of design and manufacturing. Afterwards, Prince Albert decided that the money made from the exhibition should be used to create permanent places where people could come to learn about art and science.

We know a bit about what the real Jim was like from Henry Cole's diaries. Cole often took Jim to work with him, where his behaviour was not always exemplary: 'In Museum with Jim, who barked as usual,' Cole wrote in January 1874.

Sketches of Jim by Sir Henry Cole

Cole also made a series of sketches of the scruffy-looking terrier while staying in Broadstairs in Kent in 1864. During this visit, Jim disappeared while he and Cole walked to nearby Ramsgate over the cliffs; he later arrived home safely of his own accord, to Cole's great relief.

Sir Henry Cole did create the first Christmas card in 1843; however, this was before he began his role as the first director of the museum. Alas there is no record of Jim ever visiting Buckingham Palace, but his painted dog friend does live on in the V&A — as does Jim.

Jim died in 1879. You can still visit his commemorative plaque, set into the wall of the museum he loved.

In Memory of
Jim,
Died 1879,
Aged 15 Years.
Faithful Dog of
Sir Henry Cole,
of this
Museum.

Jim's commemorative plaque
in the V&A Museum

Original illustration of

JIM

by Emma Thompson